Banscherus, J

Computer crook

Computer Crook

by J. Banscherus
translated by Ann Berge
illustrated by Ralf Butschkow

STONE ARCH BOOKS
www.stonearchbooks.com

First published in the United States in 2009
by Stone Arch Books
151 Good Counsel Drive, P.O. Box 669
Mankato, Minnesota 56002
www.stonearchbooks.com

First published by Arena Books
Rottendorfer str. 16, D-97074
Würzburg, Germany

Library of Congress Cataloging-in-Publication Data
Banscherus, Jürgen.
[Falsches Spiel und schnelle Mäuse. English]
The Computer Crook / by J. Banscherus; illustrated by Ralf Butschkow.
cm. — (Pathway Books. Klooz)
Orginally published: Falsches Spiel und schnelle Mäuse. Germany: Arena Verlag, 2003.
ISBN 978-1-4342-1218-4 (library binding)
[1. Mystery and detective stories.] I. Butschkow, Ralf, ill. II. Title.
PZ7.B22927Com 2009
[Fic]—dc22 2008031574

Summary: A violent computer game is all the rage, but no one knows who's making it. Klooz is going to stop the crooks putting out the game, but when they sabotage his computer, he's permanently offline! Can Klooz do his detective work the old-fashioned way?

Creative Director: Heather Kindseth
Graphic Designer: Kay Fraser

1 2 3 4 5 6 14 13 12 11 10 09

Printed in the United States of America

Table of contents

Chapter 1 The New Computer 5

Chapter 2 Magic Garden 13

Chapter 3 Red Stocking Cap 25

Chapter 4 Clicker 33

Chapter 5 Detective Skills 44

KLOOZ

Computer Crook

TOP SECRET

CHAPTER 1

The New Computer

One morning, my mom practically had to set off the fire alarm to wake me up.

"Didn't you sleep well?" she asked me at breakfast. I had been awake all night, but I just nodded because I was too tired to speak.

"Do you have a new case?" she asked.

"No," I said. "Today I'm getting my computer!"

Mom sighed. She wasn't happy that I was spending all of my money on a computer. She said that she could see me sitting in front of my monitor day and night, turning into a robot.

I wasn't really planning to play computer games, at least not very often. No, I needed the computer for my cases. The days when all a detective needed were his wits and a good sense of smell were over. I was the last detective in town still solving cases like they did in the Middle Ages.

That afternoon, a Salvatore's Pizza delivery car stopped in front of our house. I put down my homework and went outside to help Salvatore carry my monitor, printer, and keyboard into my room.

It was Salvatore's old business computer. He gave me a good deal on it. He said he might need my help someday.

There wasn't much room on my desk after we set everything up. "Bye, Klooz," said Salvatore. He headed toward the door. "Have fun with that thing."

I grabbed his arm. “Wait,” I said. “How do you turn this thing on?”

Salvatore patted me on the shoulder, which knocked me off my chair. Even though he’s only a few inches taller than me, he weighs at least 200 pounds more than I do.

“I can bake pizzas,” he said. “The best pizzas in the city. But I don’t understand computers. Not at all!” Then he quickly left.

A half an hour later, the problem was solved. I called Felix, one of my classmates. He brought the thing to life and showed me what I needed to do to turn it on and to get on the Internet. He said he’d help me if anything else went wrong.

So there it was. My computer. The monitor glowed, and it hummed quietly. The mouse fit into my hand like a jewel.

I was so happy, I could've cried. But I controlled myself. A detective doesn't cry, even when he is alone.

Just a week later, my computer helped me solve a case.

Sam, from my class, had a very expensive jacket. Two big guys who he didn't know stopped him on the way to school and took it from him.

Then Sam called me and asked if I could help him. His parents wanted to call the police, but I told him I would take on the case.

"Klooz is better than the police," he told his parents. Of course he was right!

Like always, I started by collecting all the facts. Sam told me that one of the robbers had called the other robber "Strubble."

At home, I turned on my computer. After a little searching, I found Strubble's website. There was a picture of him on the website, too.

Right away, I called Sam to come over and take a look. Of course, he recognized the person who had stolen his jacket right away.

Next, I sent the robber an email. I told him that we were going to call the police. The result was amazing. One day later, the jacket was hanging right outside our classroom after school.

Sam was happy. He paid me my usual fee of five packs of Carpenter's Chewing Gum. With just a little more practice with my new computer, I would be the greatest detective of all time.

CHAPTER 2

Magic Garden

My favorite chewing gum, Carpenter's, always helped me just as much as the computer did. The gum made sure that my brain was working. If I ever had trouble finding things on the Internet, the chewing gum helped me find the answer I was looking for right away.

It's no surprise that my payment from Sam was gone almost right away. I had to visit my friend Olga's newspaper stand to get more gum.

Usually, Olga was really happy to see me. I was confused when I walked up and she treated me like she would treat any of her customers.

"Can I help you?" she asked.

"One pack of Carpenter's, please," I said.

She passed the pack to me over the counter. I handed her the money.

"Anything else?" she asked without looking at me.

"What's up, Olga?" I asked back.

"Nothing," she said.

I tore open the package and put a piece of gum in my mouth. "Come on," I said. "Something's going on."

She pulled a big tissue from her pocket and blew her nose. "You never visit me anymore, Klooz," she said. "Do you have a girlfriend or something?"

"No way!" I said. "No, I have a new computer." I told her about how quickly I had been able to solve the case of the stolen jacket.

Olga listened to me carefully. I knew she wouldn't stay mad at me forever.

After I finished telling her the story, she disappeared into the newspaper stand. Soon, she returned with a glass of lemonade.

"It's on the house," she said and placed it in front of me. Then she asked, "How's everything going with you and that computer?"

"Great!" I said.

"Then I think I have a case for you," she said.

I drank the lemonade in one gulp.

"Tell me about the case," I said.

"Have you heard of a computer game called *Magic Garden*?" Olga asked me.

I hadn't ever heard of the game. Olga told me that one of her customers had found the game in her son's computer. The customer was totally shocked by the violent game.

She tried everything to figure out where her son had gotten it. But he wouldn't tell her, even when she took away his allowance and grounded him from the TV and computer.

"*Magic Garden*?" I asked. "That sounds nice enough."

"Quite the opposite!" Olga cried. "It's a very violent game. It's terrible!" She wiped her nose and added, "What kind of people would sell such awful games to children?"

I shrugged. I knew the kinds of games my friends played on their computers and Playstations. They weren't exactly sweet. But I'd never heard of a game called *Magic Garden*.

"Will you take the case?" Olga asked.

I nodded. “Will I be paid my usual fee?” I asked. “Five packs of Carpenter’s Chewing Gum?”

“You’ll get what you deserve,” Olga said. “Don’t you worry.”

First, I called Felix. He said he had heard of the game, but he had never played it himself. He didn’t know where to buy it.

"Do you have any idea who could help me?" I asked Felix.

"I don't have any idea, Klooz," he answered quickly. "They're all keeping quiet. You won't get any answers from them."

"Who are 'they'?" I asked.

Then I wished I hadn't asked that. One of the basics of being a good detective is to not ask every single question that's in your head. It freaks people out.

That's exactly what happened. Felix muttered, "I didn't say 'they.' You must have heard me wrong. That's not what I said at all." Then he quickly hung up.

He knew more than he was willing to say. I could tell.

Suddenly, Olga's case wasn't the only mystery I had to solve. I didn't understand why Felix didn't want to help me. What was he hiding?

Sometimes, when I'm stuck on a case, all I have to do is have a chat with Olga.

"Hello, Klooz," she said when I walked back to her newspaper stand. "Do you already need a new pack of Carpenter's?" she asked.

I shook my head. Then I told her about what had happened with Felix.

Olga thought about it for a while. "You have to tell Felix that you want to play this game yourself," she finally said.

"He would never believe it," I said, shaking my head. "Felix knows I work as a detective."

"Then you have to use a different name," said Olga. "Pretend to be someone else."

I laughed. "How am I supposed to do that? Am I supposed to glue a beard to my face? Everyone knows me! It won't work, Olga," I told her.

Olga crossed her arms and frowned. "Who's the detective here?" she asked. "You or me?"

Deep in thought, I went home.

My mom was working late at the hospital. I had the apartment all to myself. Like I always do when I'm stuck on a case, I got in the bathtub. I let the hot water run and started to think.

Olga was right. If I wanted to know who the mysterious "they" were, I had to pretend that I wanted to buy *Magic Garden*. I also had to pretend to be someone else. The secret group couldn't know who I was.

I got out of the tub, dried off, and got dressed. Then I called Sam. He answered right away.

"Do you have a computer?" I asked.

"Of course," Sam said.

"And an email address?" I asked.

"Yeah, Klooz, of course I do," Sam said. "Why?"

I told him what I was planning to do. I only told him what he had to know. I had to be careful. I didn't know for sure that he wasn't part of the secret group.

Ten minutes later, an email was on its way from Sam to Felix. Sam told Felix he was interested in buying *Magic Garden*. Now all we had to do was wait until Felix wrote back.

CHAPTER 3

Red Stocking Cap

A few days later, Sam got a reply to his email. He sent it to me.

The email said, "8 o'clock, City Hall fountain. Red stocking cap."

The email address was missing. Sam said he didn't know who it had come from.

That was very smart of whoever had sent the email. I could only hope that the sender of this message would show up at the city hall fountain.

Then the phone rang. It was my mother. She always called when she had to work late. And she always asked me the same questions.

"Did you do your homework? Did you clean up? Did you eat dinner? Did you feed the guinea pig? Will you go to bed early tonight?"

Finally she said, "I just got a funny call. Someone asked me if I was the mother of Klooz, the detective."

That woke me right up. "What did you say?" I asked. "Who was it?"

"I asked him who he was and why he wanted to know," she answered. "Then he hung up. What is this all about, Klooz?"

"I have no idea, Mom," I said.

I really didn't have any idea what that call could mean. Maybe it was just a new customer. But it could have also been one of the people in the mysterious secret group that Felix had mentioned.

Did they already know that I was on their trail? How could they know? Besides Felix and Sam, no one knew about my case. I decided that either Felix or Sam had to be friends with someone in the secret group.

There was no other way to explain it. I had to figure out which of them it was.

It was almost 8, so before I did anything else, I had to go to the fountain at City Hall.

On the steps of City Hall, a few skateboarders were practicing tricks. A few more feet away, there were two boys. One of them was wearing a red stocking cap.

I waited until the skateboarders left. Then I went over to the boy with the hat. The big clock on City Hall read exactly 8 o'clock.

"Here I am," I said. It was a dumb thing to say, but I didn't know what else to say.

"What do you want?" asked the boy.

FLORA
K

"Didn't you tell me to meet you here?" I asked back.

The boy stared angrily at me. "I didn't tell anyone to meet me here," he said.

I was pretty sure I was talking to the wrong guy, but I wanted to be sure. "It's about the game," I said.

"If you want to play games, go find a sandbox," said the boy with the hat. His friend laughed.

"Go! Get out of here!" the first boy said.

I stayed at the fountain for a little while longer, but no one else with a red stocking cap appeared.

Then I wondered if the note had meant that I should wear a red stocking cap.

That could be it! Why didn't I think of that sooner? Instead, I was wearing my cap with the "K" on it.

I went to go meet these guys under a false name in clothes that everyone recognizes me in. What a dumb thing to do! Now I had to start the investigation all over from the beginning.

At home, I checked my email. I had one new message.

The subject line said, "To all private detectives! Net Hunter is the unbeatable program for Internet investigation!" The email had been sent from someone named Clicker.

I could really use a program like Net Hunter, especially now that I was at a dead end with my new case. But first I needed to know who had sent me the email. I didn't know anyone named Clicker. And I knew better than to just trust anyone.

I had to find Clicker and see who he was. Hopefully, he lived here in the city. I didn't have money for travel. Besides, my mother would never allow it, especially not during the school year.

So I wrote back: "I'm very interested. Can meet at 4 o'clock tomorrow. Where? Klooz."

It didn't take very long before an email came back to me. "Time okay. Meeting place: Internet café near the art museum. Clicker."

CHAPTER 4

Clicker

I woke up a few times during the night. I kept having bad dreams about giant, dancing stocking caps.

Thousands of them marched out of my computer and walked toward me. It was terrible!

When I woke up I was covered in sweat. I only felt better after I had three glasses of milk and a piece of Carpenter's gum.

At school the next day, our teacher told us that Felix and Sam were both home sick. I knew it wasn't just chance that they were both sick. One of them had to be avoiding me. Or could both of them be part of it?

After the last bell rang, I gathered my things and walked to Olga's newspaper stand. I only had one piece of Carpenter's gum left. It was time for me to buy a new pack.

When I got there, Olga was outside the newspaper stand. She was leaning against the front of the counter with her eyes closed, enjoying the sun. I crept around the counter as quietly as possible. Then I asked, "What'll it be?"

Olga almost had a heart attack, she was so surprised. She needed a little while before she could even speak.

"Don't ever do that again, Klooz!" she shrieked. "That could have been the end of me! Never do that again, you hear? I'm not joking."

After we switched places, I bought my Carpenter's. Today, it wasn't free.

"How's the investigation?" asked Olga, after she calmed down a little.

I told her what had happened the day before. I told her about Net Hunter and Clicker, too.

"Clicker," she said. "That doesn't sound good."

"What do you mean?" I asked. "You don't like the name?"

Olga put a piece of gum in her mouth. “No, I don’t,” she said.

“Why not?” I asked.

“You remember Snake?” she asked me.

“Of course,” I said. That was a criminal I’d dealt with once.

“And Rat?” Olga asked.

I nodded. That was another crook I’d caught.

“Those were very bad guys,” said Olga. “They also had strange names.”

I touched her arm. “You’re worrying about nothing, Olga,” I said. “Clicker isn’t a bad guy. He just sells this computer program. It’s good for detectives. He’ll help me. Don’t worry about me.”

Two hours later, I was standing in front of the Internet café. I could see two guys inside, sitting at computers.

There was a counter with an espresso machine. Behind it, a woman with red hair was putting on makeup.

As I entered the café, neither man looked up. I figured neither of them was Clicker.

"Do you want to use a computer?" asked the woman behind the counter.

I shook my head. "Can I just wait here?" I asked. "I'm meeting someone named Clicker."

She laughed. "Clicker? I don't think I know anyone with that name," she said. "Would you like something to drink?"

INTERNET
CAFÉ

"Do you have milk?" I asked. To my surprise, she nodded and handed me a glass.

I had just finished my milk when a boy walked into the café. He was a few years older than me.

"Klooz?" he asked.

"Clicker?" I asked.

Clicker nodded. Then, without another word, he led me to the nearest computer. Then he pulled a disc out of his jacket pocket and put it into the computer. The program started up.

For an hour, Clicker showed me everything that could be done with his Net Hunter program. It was really amazing. The program could find banned games and sites. It could also tell who had put them on the Internet in the first place.

Finally, Clicker took the disc out of the computer and looked at me. "So, Klooz? Do you want it?" he asked.

"Well, yeah," I said. I did want it, especially if it could find *Magic Garden*.

I wanted to ask him if he could search for *Magic Garden*, but he interrupted me. "It costs 40 dollars," he said.

Then the detective in me came out. "Wait, where did you get my name?" I asked.

"From King," he answered. I knew King. I had lost a detective's duel to him once. Clicker went on, "King has been using my program for a very long time."

King used Clicker's program? That sounded good. Very good, actually. But I wasn't done yet. "Do you know the game *Magic Garden*?" I wanted to know. "It's supposed to be the most violent game ever."

Clicker shook his head. "Never heard of it, Klooz," he said. "But if it's banned, you'll find it with my program." He looked up at the clock. "Oh, I have to go," he said. "I have other customers. Do you want to buy it or not?"

I nodded. "But forty dollars is too much for me," I said. "I only have thirty."

He only hesitated for a few minutes. "Okay," he said.

CHAPTER 5

Detective Skills

When I got home, I put the disc into the computer. I typed in the words "Magic Garden."

At first, nothing happened. Then a bunch of strange numbers and symbols appeared.

Then the screen flashed a few times. Finally, the screen turned black.

I felt like my heart had stopped beating!

For the next hour, I tried everything I could think of to restart the computer. I pushed every button on the keyboard. I unplugged it and plugged it back in. Nothing worked.

I finally gave up. I put a piece of Carpenter's in my mouth. Then I poured a glass of milk and thought for a while.

There were only two possibilities. The first possibility was that Salvatore knew that his computer was about to fall apart and he sold it to me anyway.

I didn't think that was what had happened. Yes, the pizza baker was a rascal, but I didn't think he would ever sell me a piece of junk.

Besides, Mom and I were some of his best customers. We ate a lot of pizza.

Thinking about the second possibility really made me sweat. If there wasn't anything wrong with the computer, that meant someone was out to get me.

At the Internet café, everything had worked perfectly with the Net Hunter software. My computer had broken after I had typed the name of the game and pressed the search button.

Was Clicker part of the secret mysterious group? Did he set up his program to crash my computer after I typed in the words "Magic Garden"? Did he and his helpers set me up so I wouldn't find them? They locked up my computer so I couldn't do anything!

The longer I thought about it, the more sure I was that I had made a huge mistake.

Clicker had tricked me! I couldn't believe I'd given him 30 dollars. I was so mad. Clicker and his friends were about to get to know the real Klooz!

I rode my bike to Sam's house. He was really sick. He was lying in bed with a high fever. But still, he turned on his computer so that I could send an email.

I typed, "Hello, Clicker! Your program doesn't work. Please email me back. Klooz."

After a few minutes, the email came back. Sam looked at the screen. "The address doesn't exist," he said.

"Maybe I typed it in wrong," I said.

Sam shook his head. "It was typed right," he said.

The address didn't exist anymore. The boy who had called himself Clicker had obviously deleted it right after our meeting.

"What's going on, Klooz?" asked Sam.

"I'll tell you later. Get well soon!" I said and left.

Sam wasn't part of the secret group. He had no clue what was going on. I had to find Felix. He knew something. I was totally sure about that.

On the way to Felix's, I passed Olga's newspaper stand. She had just closed the window and was locking up for the day.

"Can you help me?" I asked her.

"It depends," she answered. "What do you need?"

"I need some help," I said.

"On your case?" Olga asked.

I nodded.

"You know very well that I can't say no to you," she said. "Come on, we'll take my car."

She opened the newspaper stand so that I could put my bike inside. Then we got into Olga's car and drove away.

Felix lived in a huge old house near the city park. His front yard was the size of half a football field. I asked Olga to wait in the car. Then I went up and rang the fancy doorbell.

I heard a buzzer and the door opened. A woman with long black hair was waiting inside. I offered her my hand and bowed a little.

"Felix is upstairs," said the woman. "Take the stairs. His room is the first door on the right."

I found the door to Felix's room. I went inside without knocking.

There were monitors and computers everywhere. Felix was sitting at one of the computers. He hadn't heard me come in. I could see some pretty gross things on the monitor, so I was sure he was playing *Magic Garden*.

"Hello, Felix," I said.

Felix turned around. "What are you doing here?" he asked.

"I heard you were sick," I said.

He started to turn off his computer, but I stopped him. "But I can see that you aren't sick at all," I said.

His eyes narrowed. "What do you want, Klooz?" he asked.

I sat down at his desk and put a piece of Carpenter's in my mouth. "You know exactly what I want," I said.

"I have no idea," he said.

"Really?" I said. "What would you think if I called your mother?"

Felix wiped the sweat from his forehead. "My mother? Why?" he asked, trying to stay calm.

"She should see what you're playing right now," I answered.

Felix jumped up. He was shorter and smaller than me. If he wanted to hit me, I could probably defend myself. But I hate violence. I just said, "Sit down!" And he did.

"You sent Clicker after me," I said.

"They forced me to!" he cried.

"Who are these people?" I asked. "Tell me. Or else I'll get your mother!"

Felix shrunk in his chair. "They'll destroy me," he said.

"Who are 'they'?" I asked.

"Clicker and the others cannot know that I ratted them out," Felix said. "Promise me that."

"I promise," I said. "Now tell me where I can find them."

A few minutes later, Olga and I were on our way. We followed the directions Felix had given me. Soon, we were driving out of the city. As Olga drove, we didn't talk much. We were too busy following Felix's directions.

Finally, Olga stopped in front of a garage. There was just a little bit of light coming from under the garage door.

"That's where they are," I whispered, even though no one besides Olga would have heard me.

She took a deep breath and let it out slowly. "Boy, this is exciting!" Olga said.

"You have to come with me," I said. "Please!"

"What if they hurt us?" Olga asked nervously.

I laughed, even though I wasn't feeling that brave. "We're not in a movie, Olga!" I said.

I have to admit that as we got out of the car, my legs were a little shaky. But there was no going back now. It was time to catch Clicker and his friends.

We found a door on the side of the garage and went in. Inside, we could see three computer desks.

There were three teenagers bent over keyboards. One of them was wearing a red stocking cap.

"Hello," I said.

"Good evening," said Olga.

The three turned around right away. They stared at us like we were from Mars.

The one with the red hat was Clicker. “Is that you, Klooz?” he asked.

I nodded. Then I said, “This is Olga. And now you’re going to tell us why you are selling *Magic Garden* to children.”

"What if we don't?" he asked. He and his friends stood up. They took a step toward us.

Olga pulled her cell phone out of her purse. "Stop!" she said. "Not another move, or I'll call the police!"

"Now talk!" I added.

Clicker sat down at his desk. He explained that he and his friends had been developing the *Magic Garden* game for the last two years.

At first, it was called *Kill Your Enemies*. But they couldn't find a company that would help sell a game that had a name like that.

"Everyone thought it was too violent," said Clicker.

"I can see why," I said.

Finally, they changed the name to *Magic Garden*. They sold it to kids for fifty dollars. Of course, none of the kids had that much money. But because they wanted the game so badly, they took the money from their parents.

Then Clicker and his friends had control over the kids. If the kids didn't pay him, Clicker threatened to tell the parents that the kids had stolen from them.

"Criminals!" cried Olga.

"I want all the names of all the people who bought the game," I said. "Names and addresses. Understood?"

"Okay, okay, Klooz," said Clicker.

"And I want my thirty dollars back," I continued.

Clicker nodded.

"And I want my computer working again," I added.

"That too, Klooz," Clicker agreed.

"And if I hear you've sold another game to a kid, I'm going straight to the police. Got it?" I said.

Clicker nodded quickly. "Okay," he said. "How did you find us, anyway?"

"I used some old-fashioned detective skills," I answered.

Over the next few weeks, I visited all of the kids whose names and addresses were on Clicker's list. I told them they wouldn't be threatened by anyone else.

Then I deleted the games from their computers and destroyed the discs.

A few of them almost cried, including my classmate Felix. They were really addicted to the game.

Just like he promised, Clicker brought my computer back to life. Even though he's an expert, he needed an entire afternoon to fix the thing.

After he left, I went to visit Olga. There was a long line at her newspaper stand. I had to wait a while for my turn. When I reached the front of the line, Olga passed me ten packs of Carpenter's and a glass of lemonade. "Here's your payment," she said.

"Thanks, Olga," I said. "But my payment is only five packs!"

"Five are from the customer," Olga said. "She wanted me to thank you and tell you that she'll recommend you to her friends."

"What about the other five packs?" I asked.

"Those are from me," Olga told me. "That was the most exciting thing I've done in twenty years!"

Then she put another package in front of me. "Open it," she said.

I opened the box. There was a computer game inside.

"What is this?" I asked.

Olga turned red. "I bought it earlier today, Klooz. So that you have something nice to play on your computer."

I looked closer at the game. It was called *Friends Forever.*

About the Author

Jürgen Banscherus is a worldwide phenomenon. There are almost a million Klooz books in print, and they have been translated into Spanish, Danish, Thai, Chinese, and eleven other languages. He has worked as a newspaper writer, a research scientist, and a teacher. His first book for children was published in 1985. He lives with his family in Germany.

About the Illustrator

Ralf Butschkow was born in Berlin. He works as a freelance graphic designer and illustrator, and has published more than 50 books for children. Critics have praised his work as "thoroughly enjoyable," "creatively original," and "highly recommended."

Glossary

banned (BAND)—forbidden, not allowed

basics (BAY-siks)—the most important things to know about a subject

expensive (ek-SPEN-siv)—costing a lot of money

investigation (in-vess-tuh-GAY-shuhn)—a search to learn more about something

monitor (MON-uh-tur)—the visual display part of a computer

mysterious (miss-TEER-ee-uhss)—puzzling or hard to understand

possibility (poss-uh-BIL-uh-tee)—something that might happen

recognize (REK-uhg-nize)—to see someone and know who the person is

recommend (rek-uh-MEND)—to suggest as being good

threaten (THRET-uhn)—to frighten

violent (VYE-uh-luhnt)—involving physical force

wits (WITS)—the ability to think clearly and quickly

Discussion Questions

1. Why does Klooz want a computer? Does he need the computer to solve the mystery in this book?

2. Do you think Klooz and Olga did the right thing when they went to find Clicker? What else could Klooz have done to crack the case?

3. Why did kids want to play *Magic Garden*? Can you think of anything in your own life that kids want to do even though it's dangerous?

Writing Prompts

1. Pretend that you are Klooz. Write an email to Sam telling him what happened when you and Olga went to find Clicker and his friends.

2. Olga and Klooz are friends even though Olga is older than Klooz. Write about a friend you have who is older than you.

3. This book is a mystery story. Write your own mystery story!

More Klooz for ?

Need a detective?
Call on KLOOZ!

Mystery Fans!

This smart, funny kid has a good head on his shoulders and a good brain under that baseball cap he always wears. The whole town knows that **Klooz** is clever and cool, but his friends and family know something else: **Klooz** is loyal. He never lets you down.

Internet Sites

Do you want to know more about subjects related to this book? Or are you interested in learning about other topics? Then check out FactHound, a fun, easy way to find Internet sites.

Our investigative staff has already sniffed out great sites for you!

Here's how to use FactHound:

1. Visit *www.facthound.com*
2. Select your grade level.
3. To learn more about subjects related to this book, type in the book's ISBN number: **9781434212184**.
4. Click the **Fetch It** button.

FactHound will fetch the best Internet sites for you!